Sylvia & Miz Lula Maye

Pansie Hart Flood

illustrated by

Felicia Marshall

Carolrhoda Books, Inc./Minneapolis

Carolrhoda Books, Inc.
A division of Lerner Publishing Group
241 First Avenue North
Minneapolis, MN 55401 U.S.A.

Website address: www.lernerbooks.com

Library of Congress Cataloging-in-Publication Data

Flood, Pansie Hart.
Sylvia & Miz Lula Maye / by Pansie Hart Flood ; illustrations by Felicia Marshall.
p. cm.
Summary: In 1978, ten-year-old Sylvia and her mother move to Wakeview, South Carolina, where Sylvia becomes best friends with a woman approaching her one-hundredth birthday.
ISBN: 0–87614–204–8
[1. Family life—South Carolina—Fiction. 2. Best friends—Fiction. 3. Old age—Fiction. 4. African Americans—Fiction. 5. South Carolina—Fiction.]
I. Marshall, Felicia, ill. II Title.
PZ7.F66185 Sy 2002
[Fic]—dc21 2001001615

Manufactured in the United States of America
1 2 3 4 5 6 – SB – 07 06 05 04 03 02

In memory of my beloved grandmother, whose existence
inspired me to create the character Miz Lula Maye

Pearlie Mae Reaves Wallace
1892–2000

Also, for Merrill, Jasmine, and Joey for unconditional love,
support, patience, and belief in my writing

Contents

Chapter

ONE

The Mail Chase

I thought I heard the mail truck pull off, so I leaped up from in front of the TV and ran to check the mailboxes out on Pearle Road. The brown wooden mailbox with the numbers 143 painted on the side belongs to Miz Lula Maye, the lady who lives in the house at the end of the road. The black metal mailbox with the numbers 145 belongs to me and my momma, at least it has since June. We moved into this house when my school year ended back in Jackson, Florida.

Having to move to Wakeview, South Carolina, right at the start of summer vacation was not my idea of fun. I kinda wanted to stay in Florida, but we had no choice. My momma lost her job picking oranges, so we could no longer live on the farm for orange pickers. It wasn't her fault. A lot of orange pickers were let go. Momma said she had a friend who grew up in Wakeview. So that led us here—here to this dry, hot, musky place. I guess it hasn't really mattered all that much that we moved. I didn't really have anything or anybody in Jackson, no how.

It's my job every day except Sunday to check the mailboxes. It was Monday. After dropping Momma's mail on the kitchen table, I walked down the dirt road to deliver mail to Miz Lula Maye. I've been told that the mosquitoes and gnats never sleep during the summer in Wakeview. I was in the middle of fanning away gnats with Miz Lula Maye's mail when an envelope slipped out of my hand.

As I bent down forward, reaching for the envelope, the wind hoisted it into a tumbleweed-like whirlwind. Every time I'd reach for the envelope, it would tumble away. It was like tryin' to catch a fish with your bare hands. This happened over and over and over.

So there I was, running down a dusty dirt road, bent over like the hunchback from Notre Dame, chasing one stupid piece of mail. I was really starting to get ticked off. All of a sudden, my mind told me to halt. So I did what my mind told me to do. When I stopped, the weight of my head (not sayin' that I have a big head) threw me to the ground.

There I lay, flat on my belly. My nose and lips were pressed into the dirt road like a pie in the face. Even worse, when I raised my head, I picked up the scent of some two-day-old, almost dried-up dog poop. It sat less than one measly inch away from my left hand, which held the rest of Miz Lula Maye's mail.

I was so mad! I carefully moved my hand away from the dog poop and got up. Then I stomped my foot down, capturing the evil envelope. That's when I noticed the return address. It had an interesting symbol stamped in the top left corner. In blue fancy letters it said:

The President of the United States of America
1600 Pennsylvania Avenue
Washington, DC 20500

Oh, my God! I thought. Miz Lula Maye must be in some deep trouble to be getting mail from the president.

I ran the entire rest of the way down to Miz Lula Maye's house. She lives in a white wooden farmhouse that's probably as old as she is. Her screen door was unlocked (as usual). So I invited myself in.

"Miz Lula Maye, your mail is here!" I yelled. "And guess what? You got something from the president! The president of the United States!"

Miz Lula Maye entered into the kitchen where I was standing sweaty and anxious to hand her the envelope. I slung the rest of her mail on the kitchen counter.

"What did you say, Sylvia?" said Miz Lula Maye.

"You've got some mail from the White House!" I yelled again, but this time even louder.

"Well, what's it about?" Miz Lula Maye asked calmly.

We sat at the kitchen table while I carefully opened the envelope and read the letter. "Oh, my George!" I shouted. "Miz Lula Maye, this letter really is from the president, *our* president! He wrote this letter to wish you a happy one-hundredth birthday!" I looked up at Miz Lula Maye with a glorifying smile. She was grinning from ear to ear.

"Sylvia, I sho' is honored to get a letter from the president," Miz Lula Maye said, chuckling. "It's one thing to see a hundred years. But Lord, this sho' puts the icin' on the cake."

I couldn't believe I was holding paper that had been touched by the president. I wondered if he had licked the envelope with his spit. I rubbed the paper and smelled the envelope to see if I could pick up the scent of Mr. President's spit or maybe his cologne. Unfortunately, all I could smell was nothing but paper. I positioned my eyes real close to the paper. I licked my pointer finger and rubbed the signature to see if it was real ink or just some fake signature stamped with a rubber stamp. It didn't smear, but I could tell it was indeed a true signature. This was from the real McCoy.

Miz Lula Maye went and got the iron and ironing board. After letting the iron heat up, she ironed the letter flat. I'd never seen anyone iron paper before. Then she got a picture frame from a drawer in her coffee table and carefully placed the letter in the frame. After wiping off the glass in the frame, she placed it on her coffee table for everyone to see as soon as they entered through her front door.

I wonder, how did Mr. President find out about Miz Lula Maye's birthday? I guess the president knows everything. He has to know everything 'cause he's in charge.

"Miz Lula Maye, do you think the president can send me a letter when I turn eleven?" I asked.

"Well, I don't know. When you turnin' eleven?" questioned Miz Lula Maye as she settled into her favorite armchair.

"In September! September 29, 1967, is when I was born," I told her.

"Umph! Time sho' does fly—1967 seems like yesterday," Miz Lula Maye said.

"It doesn't to me," I said. "Seems like it's takin' me forever to turn eleven. What year were you born in, Miz Lula Maye?" I asked. But Miz Lula Maye was starting to doze off into her late afternoon nap.

"Let's see now," I whispered to myself. "If you were born one hundred years ago and it's 1978, then you should've been born in 18 . . . um . . . 1878. Wow!"

I looked at Miz Lula Maye. She was asleep. She nodded her head with a happy-peaceful lookin' kinda smile that reminded me of a white bunny rabbit I got for Easter last year. Bunny! Yeah, Bunny. That's what I named the rabbit. A perfect happy-peaceful smile stitched with pink silky thread outlined Bunny's mouth. That's what Miz Lula Maye's smile looked like.

Miz Lula Maye's hair is long, silky, and straight. She wears it in two long ponytails with a part straight down the middle of her head. Her hair is the exact color of shiny pearls. Not fake pearls, but real ones. Even though I ain't never touched her hair, it's soft as cotton, I know. I can tell by the way it curls up at the ends.

It's amazing, but Miz Lula Maye doesn't look anywhere near a hundred. She barely has wrinkles.

Her beautiful brown skin is practically as smooth as my momma's. I wonder if Miz Lula Maye gots any Indian in her? With her high cheekbones and ponytails, she kinda looks like an Indian woman.

I'm so proud of her. I thought about it while I tiptoed out the door. Even though I've only known her for a few weeks, I can already feel that she is very special. I feel special just knowing her.

Chapter 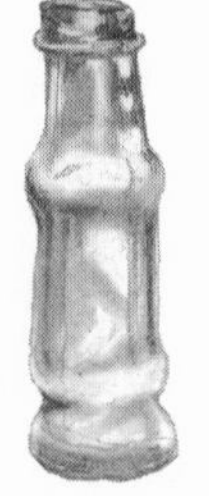 TWO

At the House with Momma

On my way back to the house, I made sure I stayed on the side of the dirt road away from that stinking dog poop. One close encounter with dog poop a day is enough.

There are only three houses on Pearle Road, which is mostly surrounded by Miz Lula Maye's fields. Miz Lula Maye's house sits by itself at the end of the road. At about the halfway point is Jack Jr.'s house. He's Miz Lula Maye's nephew, which seems strange to me 'cause he is old enough to be my grandpa. Momma and me lives at the start of Pearle Road. Across the street from us is a nightclub called the Juke Joint that Jack Jr. runs.

Jack Jr. also helps out Miz Lula Maye by hiring hands to work in her fields.

It's pretty quiet around here. If Miz Lula Maye wasn't around, I wouldn't have nobody to talk with during the day. Momma leaves for work in the pepper fields before I wakes up in the morning. It's hot, hard work. Nevertheless, we's lucky, 'cause Miz Lula Maye is letting us stay in this house for a little of nothing. At least, that's what my momma says.

Our screen door is missing its springs. I slammed the door behind me just to make some noise in the quiet house. The wind was blowing through the window over the kitchen sink. It made the curtains sway back and forth just like a ghost—a ghost all covered with brown roosters, black cows, pink pigs, and baskets filled with fruits and vegetables. I was starting to feel a little spooked.

"KAPOW!" I yelled. I squashed a huge horsefly with my bare hand on the windowsill and got green fly guts all over my hand. "Oh, how gross!" I said, disgusted.

I washed my hands at the sink over yesterday's

dishes. "I really should wash these dirty dishes," I said to myself. But then I decided to wait until after dinner.

There was nothin' much to do in the kitchen, so I walked into the practically empty front room. A TV, one chair that belongs in the kitchen, an olive green couch, and a couple of boxes of records were all positioned in the middle of the room. Looks more like we's movin' out instead of in.

I decided to turn on the TV to pass away time. Right about then, I heard the screen door slam shut. It scared the heck out of me, but then I realized it was my momma.

"Hey, girl!" said Momma.

"Hey, Momma!" I said with a sigh of relief. "I'm glad it's you."

"Who else would it be?" Momma said, looking at me funny.

"I have no idea," I said, following Momma into her bedroom.

After Momma showered and changed clothes, we both went into the kitchen to figure out what to cook for dinner. Since it's just the two of us, dinner is usually very quick and simple.

We decided on BLTs. I smeared mayonnaise on four slices of light bread while Momma fried the bacon in the frying pan. Oh no, excuse me, the "spider." Miz Lula Maye calls a black frying pan a spider. And bread ain't just called bread, it's called light bread. Some things I don't question, I just go along with them and smile.

I sprinkled salt and black pepper over the mayo and added some lettuce and two slices of tomato. Straight from the spider, my mom laid the hot, sizzling, crispy bacon on top. I poured a little hot sauce over the bacon, then closed up the sandwiches with a piece of light bread.

My mom gave me a sassy lookin' tired smile and said, "Look at you, girl, putting hot sauce on stuff. Since when did you start liking hot sauce?" I smiled and giggled, then I took a bite and almost choked. I got strangled 'cause I put too much hot sauce on my sandwich. My mouth was on fire! Momma grabbed my glass of iced water and shoved it into my mouth. I was burning up, but it was funny. It was so funny, we both fell out laughing.

After I got myself back together, I finally said

what I had started to say before I got so tickled from getting strangled. "Miz Lula Maye introduced me to hot sauce. She uses it in a lot of her recipes. She even makes her own hot sauce, but I guess it ain't as strong as the store-bought kind."

Momma seemed to be in a good mood, at least she was until she looked at the mail. She picked up one of the envelopes and saw that the back flap was partially lifted up. "Sylvia," she said in a very low, stern voice, "were you trying to open my mail?"

I didn't know what she was talking about. I don't read her mail, I just deliver it. "No, Momma. I'd never do that!" I said. Then I asked in a cute little innocent sounding voice, "Who's the letter from?" Why oh why did I ask that? Now she'd think I'd been snooping for sure. I thought I was dead meat and cold busted.

Momma plunged onto the couch and stretched out with an exhausted sigh. "It's not important," she said. I should have expected that. Momma considers most things that I want to know to be private. I decided to be smart about this discussion and ask no further questions.

Momma nodded in and out as we watched the news. I was so bored. If it wasn't so dark around these parts, I'd have walked down to Miz Lula Maye's, but not in this lifetime. There's way too many wild things creeping around at night, crossing the dirt road.

My momma, also known as Marie Freeman, is barely thirty, but sometimes she seems so old. She works so hard and hasn't taken in any company in years. Times are kinda tough this summer. Well, actually, times always seem to be tough, at least for my mom. Sometimes I think she's been cursed with bad luck.

My dad died when I was barely two years old. I don't remember him at all. We move around throughout the year. Momma is always trying to find work so we can have a roof over our heads. I wish I was old enough to get a job, but not in the fields.

Last weekend, I asked my momma why didn't she ever go over to the club across the road. She claimed she ain't got the energy to waste shakin' her hips around on some hard, cold concrete dance floor. Then she changed the topic (which is something she is real good at doing when she doesn't want to talk about something).

I went to bed leaving Momma on the couch knocked out asleep. Later she came to my bedroom door before closing up the house and asked me if I had met any kids my age yet. I told her no, then pretended to be sleepy. Momma sat on the edge of my bed. "You really like hanging out with that old lady?" she asked.

I got defensive real quick and said, "What do you mean? What's wrong with being friends with an old lady? She makes me feel alive! We have fun together doin' things and talkin'! I like spendin' time with Miz Lula Maye—besides, she doesn't even act old!"

Unfortunately, I went to sleep angry at my momma. She doesn't mind asking you questions and expecting answers, but oh, let somebody like me ask her a question. I get so mad when she dances around questions that she doesn't want me to know the answers to. I wish. I wish . . . I don't know what I wish, but I do wish I knew more about my life and her life than I know.

I mean, most kids know about their folks, folks

like their grandparents, aunts, uncles, cousins. But me, I don't really know any of my family. I've seen a (as in one) picture of my mother's parents. They both died in a house fire when my mom was five years old. She was rescued by neighbors, then placed in foster care. She doesn't really have any other family, or at least that I know of.

The other day, I asked Miz Lula Maye about my momma being so close to herself and not trying to be with or find her own relatives. Miz Lula Maye said that sometimes people just get used to being alone 'cause it's easy and not complicated. Miz Lula Maye asked me to be patient with my momma and to just love her anyhow. "I sense your momma's in need of healin' from something. I'll pray for her and a change will be soon to come. You'll see!" Miz Lula Maye said that and I believe her.

I love Miz Lula Maye. Sometimes the things she says and the way she says things sound so perfect and smart. I feel like we's somehow connected by some kind of inside spirit. I get chills in my arms and shoulders sometimes when we have our private talks. It's like she is teaching me so much stuff and I ain't even in school.

Chapter  THREE

Mr. Window Cat

It was another hot, muggy day. Every time I complain about it being too hot, Miz Lula Maye says, "Girl, it ain't even hot yet. It's gonna get even hotter." I'm used to heat, but this is bad. It's the middle of July, and I'm thinking, Lord, if it gets any hotter, I don't want to see August.

Miz Lula Maye didn't have any mail today. I just dropped by to check on her. Sometimes I spends the entire day with Miz Lula Maye. It don't matter to me that she's so old. She is old, very old, and she would probably be lonely if it wasn't for me stopping by to drop off her mail. Anyway, I just like her company, and I think she likes my company the same.

As I walked down the road towards Miz Lula Maye's house, I could see that she was sitting on her front porch along with her nine, or maybe twelve, cats. The reason why I say nine or twelve is 'cause sometimes the numbers change. Miz Lula Maye loves cats and cats love Miz Lula Maye. Jack Jr. is always saying that his auntie has too many cats. But she doesn't care. Sometimes a few extra cats come and stay for a spell, then leaves. Overall, you can pretty much expect at least nine permanent cats to be hangin' around.

As I approached Miz Lula Maye's porch, a big gust of wind out from nowhere made me lose my balance. I kinda tripped and stumbled up the steps. My silly moves tickled Miz Lula Maye. "You need more meat on your skinny little bones," she said laughing. "The wind shouldn't be blowin' people around unless it's a hurricane."

At first I felt so embarrassed, but then it also got funny to me. There I was, a ten-year-old girl,

being helped up by a lady who would soon be turning a hundred. Looking at Miz Lula Maye laugh with very few teeth was also real funny. In the midst of all the laughing, we both got up and went inside.

Miz Lula Maye fixed me a ham sandwich. This lady really knows how to cook. I guess she should. Anybody who's been cooking almost, probably about ninety-two years ought to be good.

Her bread is the best! She butters and toasts all of her bread in a small spider. Sometimes she makes sugar toast for a snack. She even taught me how to make sugar toast. First, lay your slices of light bread on a cookie sheet. Then rub butter over the bread. Then put it in the oven for a minute or two (just long enough to let the butter melt). Then take it out of the oven and sprinkle sugar all over the slices. Turn the oven up higher or to the broil setting, then put the bread back in the oven and let it cook for about two more minutes. When the bread looks toasted and brown, take it out of the oven.

Miz Lula Maye says it's important to stand right at the oven door when you cook it 'cause sometimes when you broil things, they cook super fast. And no one likes burnt sugar toast, 'cause when sugar burns, it gets really hard. It tastes like burnt candy. Yuk! It's awful!

After lunch, I helped Miz Lula Maye clean up the kitchen. At my house, we just put the dishes in the sink. They sit there until somebody (usually me) gets tired of looking at the pile of dirty dishes. Sometimes I wash dishes so much, I pretend it's my job. Unfortunately, I work for free. But in Miz Lula Maye's kitchen, dirty dishes are unheard of. Her kitchen is always spotless. If you use a glass or dish, she expects you to wash it immediately after using it. And after every meal, somebody from the eating table has to sweep. Another thing about Miz Lula Maye and her kitchen is that as much as she loves her cats, they don't eat in her kitchen. Ha-ha! Those creepy, lazy cats have to eat out on the back porch.

Cats have to be the luckiest animals in the world. They don't do anything but eat, sleep, and lazy around all day, every day. When it's cold or rainy outside, they gets to come inside the house. Even when it's too hot, Miz Lula Maye lets 'em come inside. I don't get it! She treats those cats like people. What a life! These cats ain't just lucky, they're smart, too. You can look at 'em and they looks like they are tryin' to read your mind. That's why I don't particularly like cats.

I don't know much about cats or any animals. I've never had a pet. I don't know the real animal names for these cats, and I don't think Miz Lula Maye does, either. Nevertheless, Miz Lula Maye has given her cats some other easy-to-remember names.

Mr. Window Cat was named 'cause he likes sitting on windowsills. Miz Step Cat and Little Miz Step Cat (her baby daughter) enjoy napping right in everybody's way in the middle of the porch steps. Do they move when you need to come up or go down the steps? No! They think you're supposed to step over 'em or go around. Now, if that ain't spoiled, I don't know what is. I personally can't believe nobody has ever accidentally stepped on one of Miz or Little Miz Step Cat's tails. Hum. That's very interesting, interesting indeed. I just might need to do something about that. . . .

Miz Porch Cat likes sitting anywhere on the porch. Rarely does she leave the porch unless it involves fetching food. Mr. Rug Cat owns the rug in front of the door. He is almost like a watchdog. You have to pass over Mr. Rug Cat both coming and going. Mr. Rug Cat is simply one more cat who thinks he is in charge. Miz Chair Cat prefers lounging in a rocking chair, and yes, she likes to be rocked.

Mr. Corner Cat likes snuggling up in any corner of the porch. Now, he does look cute, especially when he curls up like the letter C. Mr. Rail Cat enjoys climbing and playing on the railings that outline Miz Lula Maye's porch. Mr. Rail Cat is super hyper! He makes me more nervous than any of the other cats 'cause he moves constantly and almost silently at the same time. You don't hear him until you see him flyin' across your lap to the next landing spot. It drives me nuts. And most definitely, he knows perfectly well what he is doing.

Miz Basket Cat is the prettiest of all Miz Lula Maye's cats. Her fur is fluffy and long. She is pure white, like a snowball. Her face almost looks like a pancake, and her eyes are baby blue-green. Miz Basket Cat lives in a large straw basket that Miz Lula Maye purchased years ago for picking cucumbers. If Miz Lula Maye was to surprisingly give me one of her cats, I'd hope for it to be Miz Basket Cat. And I'd want Miz Basket Cat and Mr. Corner Cat to get married and have babies.

When we sat down to watch TV, I kept hearing a weird sound. Miz Lula Maye said it was just her window cat scratching at the windowsill. Then all of a sudden, there was a THUD and the loudest screech. I jumped up and poked my head out the door. At first I couldn't quite see what was the matter. Then I saw the blood.

"There's blood, Miz Lula Maye!" I yelled.

She hopped up and ran to the door quicker than any near hundred-year-old person on earth. "Where at, child?" she said.

"Over there at that window!" I shouted. Lord, Miz Lula Maye's window cat was stuck. His tail was stuck under the window. Cat blood was dripping down the wall.

I slowly and carefully raised the window. I really didn't want to get any cat blood on my hands or clothes. Miz Lula Maye stood there with her arms stretched out. Mr. Window Cat leaped into her arms as if he had come back home from a war.

We took Mr. Window Cat around to the back of the house and rinsed off his tail at the water pump. I held Mr. Window Cat tight so he wouldn't run off, and Miz Lula Maye scooped up some mud and gently patted it on the wound. This was kinda gross and fun at the same time. I love playing hospital.

While Miz Lula Maye was in the house looking for cloth scraps, I took it upon myself to give Mr. Window Cat an examination. The first question I asked was, "Mr. Window Cat, how long were you stuck in the window?" Mr. Window Cat looked at me as if he would curse me out, if he could curse. So then I asked him to open his mouth and say ahh. Next, I looked in both ears. Then I asked a silly question that made me giggle out of control. "Mr. Window Cat," I said, "can you wiggle your tail?" I laughed so loud that folks in North Carolina could hear me. "Well, my recommendation is that your tail is broken," I said to Mr. Window Cat in a serious voice.

"That's a good diagnosis," said Miz Lula Maye. I didn't even know she was standing there. I felt stupid for the second time on the same day.

Miz Lula Maye had found some pieces of material to bandage up Mr. Window Cat's tail. She wrapped it like a pro, as if she had done this before. The bandages made his tail look stiff and three times bigger than it was.

After cleaning up the operating room, I helped Miz Lula Maye scrub the porch. She went into the kitchen and got some detergent to keep the blood from leaving a permanent stain. She said the detergent would also kill the scent and keep the buzzards away.

Miz Lula Maye and I took a nap after all the excitement and cleaning. The wooden swing on her front porch is the best nap-taking spot in town. As I drifted off into a much needed and deserved sleep, my last thought was that I was surprised I hadn't thrown up that delicious ham sandwich.

Chapter FOUR

Miz Lula Maye's Party

Every weekend the Lord brings, the club across the road from my house packs in hundreds of people. Folks from North Carolina come from hours away just to shake their booties at the Juke Joint. Cars squeeze into the dirt parking lot like smelly sardines in a can. You'd think this was somewhere famous, like New York City or Hollywood.

Cars also outline Pearle Road all the way to Miz Lula Maye's house. It's pitch-black dark around here at night. If you're not familiar with the road, there's no way to know that there are deep ditches on both sides. Just about every week, a few cars get stuck in the ditch. Miz Lula Maye says that's our initiation for newcomers and a way for the Lord to keep drunks off the road.

It never fails. The drunks always get stuck in the ditches when they try to leave. The nearest tow truck is about twenty minutes away. Plus you need to include time for someone to get up out of their bed, get dressed, and drive to Wakeview. It usually takes about a good two hours for a car to be pulled out of the ditch. By that time, the drunks have had time to sober up a bit before getting on the road.

Normally on Friday nights, the Juke Joint is full of grown-ups eating, drinking, smoking, laughing, talking loud, and dancing. One hour before the club opens, the smell of hot grease frying fresh fish and chicken fills the air. If there's a live band, the drummer would be warming up by now. If there's a DJ, you can hear the music blasting for miles down the road.

There's this one DJ who is a regular at the Juke Joint. He is known as "DJ Hot." When the doors open at eight o'clock, he always starts his night off by sayin' the same old corny stuff, the same old way. He says, "Testing, one, two, three, testing, testing (pause for a minute). Okay, folks, are you ready to P-A-R-T-Y, party? It's gonna get H-O-T, hot, hot, hot, 'cause the Juke Joint is the S-P-O-T, spot, spot, spot to party with BIG DADDY D . . . J . . . HOT!" Then he turns on a siren that sounds like a fire truck.

This Friday night, things were different. This Friday, July 21, 1978, Miz Lula Maye turned one hundred years old, and her family threw her a party at the Juke Joint. Miz Lula Maye's family started rolling in 'bout noon. I watched cars kick up clouds of dust along Pearle Road all day.

I'd known about the party for a while, but I was too shy (that's hard to believe, I know, but it's true) to ask if I could come. Luckily, I didn't have to.

On Thursday, Miz Lula Maye said, "Sylvia, you's my best friend, so you gots to come to my party."

I smiled the biggest smile and said, "Who me? For real?"

"That's right," she said. "And your momma's invited, too."

Then I asked, "Miz Lula Maye, where your peoples from?"

Miz Lula Maye sighed. "Sylvia, childs, my childrens headed north soon as they was old enough to be out on their own. Work up North was easier to come by. Some lives in Virginia, D.C., Philly, Jersey, and Connecticut. I gots a lot of cousins who live as close as North Carolina, right next door to Wakeview. So you'll get to meet folks from here and yonder."

Miz Lula Maye told me she was expecting all six of her kids, plus a slew of grands and great-grands to come in. Miz Lula Maye's children handled all the inviting. Jack Jr. handled all the other arrangements, like food, music, and settin' up the Juke Joint.

On Friday night, I dressed up in the nicest sundress I've got. I even wiped off my dusty sandals with the wooden soles. Plus I lotioned my ashy legs and elbows with some of Momma's lotion that smells like perfume. On top of all that, I combed and brushed my hair into two new ponytails.

Momma didn't come to the party. She decided

to work late for a couple of extra ducketts. (At least, so she claims.) Me knowing Momma the way I do, she probably decided to work late to keep from havin' a good time.

Once I got to the Juke Joint, I did kinda wish Momma had come. I felt a little weird standing there with practically a hundred folks I don't even know. To distract myself, I took a good look around the place. I'd never been all the way inside before. I'd only peeked in the door.

This building that is now a nightclub used to be a church. I'm told that many years ago, a group of drunk young boys came through and set it on fire. The church practically burned to the ground. I'm also told that everybody knew who set the fire, but no one ever spoke out. The pastor and his congregation from Wakeview Missionary Baptist Church did not want to rebuild in the same spot. They all believed the ground had been poisoned by the devils who set the fire. So they set up church in a house about two miles down the road.

Jack Jr. got the benches to make his booths from the burnt-up church. He painted the church pews with some ugly shiny red paint. Of all colors, he chose red. He even kept the church collection tables to use at the front doors for taking up money for the club's cover charge. Even worse, stained glass windows—yes, from the old church—divide the dance area from the kitchen. I noticed that two huge blue freezer boxes with the word *Cola* written in red on the side sat under the stained glass windows. My mouth was so dry, I could have used something to drink right about then.

"Shh! Five, four, three, two, one . . . Surprise!" everyone shouted.

Miz Lula Maye was escorted in by Jack Jr. She pretended to be surprised, but everyone knew she wasn't. Miz Lula Maye had informed her children at her ninety-eighth birthday party that she wanted 'em to give her a party every year for the rest of her life. So that is exactly what they've been doing. I think it's great. Most people don't make it to their nineties. My dad didn't.

Everybody gathered around Miz Lula Maye to sing the happy birthday song. Miz Lula Maye looked great in her sky blue polyester pants suit and cream wide-rim straw church hat. That hat was bad! It had a blue band of material around the rim that matched her pants suit to a T. Miz Lula Maye's black cat-eye shaped eyeglasses made her look sophisticated. She was truly indeed dressed sharp that night. Yes, indeed.

After we sang to Miz Lula Maye, she stood up and prayed for us. It was amazing. I'm tellin' ya, that's just how she is. Then she slowly leaned over her cake adorned with one hundred flaming candles, took a long, deep breath and blew 'em out. It only took her a few tries to get all the candles blown out. Everybody clapped, cheered, and shouted.

I still can't believe what happened next. I was kinda hiding in the back behind people, but Miz Lula Maye signaled for me, Sylvia Freeman, to come over to her table. So I squeezed through the crowd and walked over to see what she wanted. Miz Lula Maye cut the first slice of her cake, put it on a plate, and handed it to me. Then she whispered in my ear, "Child, you needs to eat to get some meat on your bones. Thanks

for comin' to my party." I raised my head with the biggest grin. I felt like Miz Lula Maye had wrapped me up in a warm quilt.

Folks started taking group pictures. That's when I met Miz Peaches. Miz Lula Maye waved her hand, signaling for me to join in with a picture. She gently rested her hands on my shoulders and said, "Sylvia, I want you to meet my youngest daughter, Peaches."

"Has my momma gotten you in her kitchen yet?" asked Peaches.

"Sure has," I said with a giggle. "How did you know?"

Peaches said, "If you're a girl hanging out with my momma, she's gonna teach you how to cook. It's her favorite thing. If you hang around long enough, she'll teach you how to do some of any and everything. Momma should have been a teacher. Well, in a way, a home teacher is really what she was."

"Was?" I said. "She still is, and a good one at that."

Miz Peaches and Miz Lula Maye ended up introducing me to so many people, I can't even begin to remember names. They helped me to feel so welcomed, I almost forgot I was in a room full of people I didn't know.

Everyone had plenty of birthday cake, collard greens, field peas with okra, rice, yellow potato salad, cornbread, fried catfish, ham, and fried chicken. Then Miz Lula Maye opened her gifts.

This may seem strange, but all of her gifts were cards in envelopes. Every year, Miz Lula Maye requests no gifts. So people bring cards, and yes, most of the cards have money tucked inside.

I tried counting all the money but lost count after I got to two hundred seventy-five dollars. For every card Miz Lula Maye opened, whether it had money in it or not, she chuckled and said, "Lord, I thank you so much!" It took so long for Miz Lula Maye to open all of her birthday cards that people stopped watching and started talking, dancing, and having a real good time. I stuck with her, though.

When Miz Lula Maye finally finished, she stood up and shouted, "Thank you everyone, and I'll be lookin' forward to doin' this with you all again next year!" She bid everyone good night and blessings from God, then left through a line-up of hugs and kisses from all her guests.

After Miz Lula Maye left, I went home, too. Even though I was stuffed full as a tick, I took home a plate piled high with birthday cake, fried chicken, and yellow potato salad. Miz Lula Maye would have been proud of me and my extra plate of food. In all honesty, though, I brought most of the food home to my mom, but she was already in bed asleep.

As I lay in my bed fully awake, I savored all the memories of Miz Lula Maye's one-hundredth surprise (but not really) birthday party. Even though I just met all of those people, they treated me like I was one of them, like I was a member of their family. One time back in Florida, when Momma got tired of me asking her questions about her family, she said, "You can't miss what you ain't never had." But as far as I'm concerned, I think you can.

I hope and pray that Miz Lula Maye will have many, many more birthdays and birthday parties like the one I attended at the Juke Joint. The president should have been there. He would have had a blast. Oh well, that's his loss.

Chapter FIVE

The Disappearance

The day after the party, I didn't wake up until just before noon. The mailman had already come and gone. The mail comes early on Saturdays. I don't know why. My only guess is that the mailman drives faster so he can start his weekend sooner.

I hopped out of bed once I realized I had slept half the day away. I ran out of the house in my pj's to get the mail. More birthday cards had arrived for Miz Lula Maye. I was so anxious to chat with Miz Lula Maye about the party that I headed straight down the road without going back inside to get dressed.

When I stuck my head in Miz Lula Maye's screen door, I noticed she had displayed all of her birthday cards in the front room. The mantle was covered with cards. Her long coffee table in front of the couch was covered with cards. The three end tables were all covered with cards. Cards were everywhere! It was so beautiful.

I didn't see Miz Lula Maye, but I could hear her voice in the distance. I found her outside in the garden. She was almost crying. I began to feel scared and nervous. I'd never seen her like this before. Since she is one hundred years old, my first thought was that she was sick or feeling like she was about to die.

"What's wrong, Miz Lula Maye?" I asked.

"All of my cats is gone!" Miz Lula Maye said. "I been callin' for 'em all morning. But I ain't seen no signs of any of my babies."

Miz Lula Maye is something about her cats. She loves 'em almost as much as she loves her own children. Furthermore, for her cats to skip a meal (like breakfast) is unheard of and had simply never happened before, according to Miz Lula Maye.

I put my arms around Miz Lula Maye and gave her a big bear hug. "They'll be back before it gets dark," I said. But in my own mind I thought, how and where in God's name will I find nine new cats?

I went into the kitchen to fetch Miz Lula Maye a cold glass of iced tea. When I came back outside, Miz Lula Maye was sitting in her rocking chair. She looked strange, serious, determined, and almost possessed. This was turning out to be a rather peculiar day. Not only did I still have on my pj's and hadn't brushed my teeth or washed my face. But nine cats were missing and Miz Lula Maye was not acting like herself. What next?

The glass was freezing my fingers, so I handed it to Miz Lula Maye. She took one long chug-a-lug of her iced tea. Then she set her glass on the porch and got up out of her rocking chair so fast it almost rocked over. "I've got it!" she said. "I know where to look for my cats!" In a second, she was down the stairs and heading for the road.

I, being the curious type, asked, "Where are you headed?"

Miz Lula Maye turned around towards me and

(walking backwards) said, "I'm gonna whip Jack Jr.'s butt if he has done anything with my cats!"

I thought Miz Lula Maye might be on the right track, 'cause I had heard Jack Jr. teasing her about the cats. He said he was gonna kidnap 'em and take 'em to another town. I was a potential witness to this cat crime and possibly a human crime.

Miz Lula Maye was polite enough to knock at the door of Jack Jr.'s house. When there was no answer, she stepped off the porch and pulled a switch from one of his shrubs. Next, she went back to the door and yelled, "Jack Jr., boy, open this here door before I open it myself!" But there was still no answer.

"He ain't home, Miz Lula Maye," I said.

"I reckon not," Miz Lula Maye said quietly. Then she gave me a smile like a kid sneakin' cookies from the kitchen. "Good," she whispered. "Let's go in. His place probably needs a woman's touch, anyhow."

No, she didn't! Yes sir, she did! Yes, we did! She and I plundered through Jack Jr.'s house looking for cat clues. We ran across some interesting clues, but none had anything to do with Miz Lula Maye's nine cats.

We looked in the kitchen and the living room. We checked in Jack Jr.'s bedroom and his bathroom. Then suddenly, Miz Lula Maye placed her finger over her lips and motioned for me to keep quiet. Slowly and quietly, I moved toward Miz Lula Maye. She pointed at a door in the hallway.

"Did you open that door?" Miz Lula Maye whispered.

"No! Why?" I whispered back.

"'Cause, it was closed just a minute ago," she said. "Shh, I think Jack Jr. is hidin' behind that door."

I couldn't stand it. I was so excited. Bustin' Jack Jr. was gonna be some kinda funny. Together we inched over to the door and jerked it open as fast as we could.

"Lord, Jesus!" I shouted. "It's a woo-man!"

"Lydia, get yourself out from behind this here door!" Miz Lula Maye yelled. "What you doin' up in Jack Jr.'s house anyway, especially and he ain't even here?"

Lydia didn't answer. She just stood there

lookin' stupid. I thought she was DJ Hot's girl-friend. But I guess maybe not, not anymore.

Miz Lula Maye questioned Lydia about Jack's whereabouts. Lydia was so stunned in shock, she could barely speak. She mumbled and pointed in the direction of the Juke Joint. Without paying Lydia any more mind, Miz Lula Maye headed out the door with the switch still in her hand. From the look on her face, I knew no one better get in her way.

Jack Jr. might be a grown man, but on this here day, I was sure he was gonna get a whippin', and my eyes were ready to watch. This was better than anything on television. Of course, I followed Miz Lula Maye to assist if necessary in her cat quest.

The back door area at the Juke Joint was stinkin' bad 'cause Jack Jr. was too lazy to burn the trash from Miz Lula Maye's party. Those fish heads and chicken parts were smellin' up something. We walked around front and went in through the front door of the building instead.

When the Juke Joint is empty, it sure is dreary and ugly on the inside. The floor is made of cold gray concrete, and the red church pews could use some paint. The place was silent and it was dark—except for a beam of light peeking through a crack in the door and spotlighting Jack Jr., asleep in a booth.

When Miz Lula Maye saw Jack Jr., she asked me if I was thirsty. I knew it was to get me out of the way, but I didn't care. Who in their right mind would pass up the chance to drink an ice, ice cold soda pop? The freezers were packed full of cola, grape, strawberry, and orange soda pop.

While I was busy choosing a soda, Miz Lula Maye was waking up Jack Jr. with her whippin' switch. I finally settled for a cola. I also grabbed a small pack of salted, shelled peanuts. Then I settled into the back corner booth. I poured about half of the peanuts into my soda bottle. I was no longer bothered by the poor décor of the Juke Joint. I was in soda pop heaven, sipping on cola and munching on cola-soaked peanuts.

I heard a yelp and looked across the room to see Jack Jr. quickly sliding out of his booth with his hands protecting his head. Miz Lula Maye went after him, swinging the switch. He ran towards the

stained glass windows shouting, "I ain't got your smelly cats, I swear, honest to God!"

"Don't you use the Lord's name in vain, boy!" yelled Miz Lula Maye. "What did you do with my cats? Tell me, tell me now and stop your playin'!" As Jack Jr. was saying that he would put his hand on the Bible and swear he hadn't done anything with the cats, a mellow meow came from between his legs. There, wagging at Jack Jr.'s feet, was the bandaged tail of Mr. Window Cat.

Jack Jr. shrunk to the size of one of Snow White's dwarfs. He was speechless, stupid, and stunned. Miz Lula Maye pushed Jack Jr. to the side and called him a lyin' fool. She headed through the kitchen and stepped out the back screen door. There, in the garbage pit, lay the eight other cats, stuffed, dirty, and asleep. All those fish heads were now fish bones and all those chicken parts had become chicken bones.

Miz Lula Maye was so happy to find her babies. "Lord, thank you, Jesus, for helping me find my cats," she said. Then in the same breath, she turned around and yelled, "Jack Jr., boy, go and tell that girl Lydia to get out of your house.

You knows good and well that she ain't got no business bein' there if you ain't home!"

That's when I realized I'd better get goin' myself. It had already been quite a day, and there I was, still in my pj's! I figured folks around me would probably appreciate it if I'd take a bath and brush my teeth. I laughed about Jack Jr. and those stupid, silly cats all the way home.

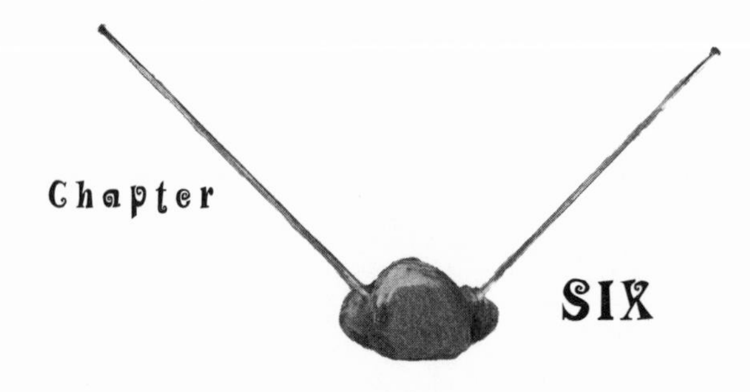

Chapter SIX

A Stormy Night

That afternoon, there was nothing on TV and Momma was too tired to talk, as usual. I went outside and checked out Miz Lula Maye's mailbox to see if I'd missed anything. I figured that even junk mail would give me an excuse to go back over to Miz Lula Maye's house and see what she was doing. The mailbox was empty. I started walking slowly down the road toward Miz Lula Maye's house anyway.

It was steamy and muggy outside. I probably

had at least ten gnats stuck to the skin on my neck. The frogs, crickets, and other loud mouth insects were making as much noise as they could possibly make.

Sprigs of what Miz Lula Maye calls lavender were poking above the other weeds and wildflowers along the side of the road. They smelled like perfume. I decided that since I didn't have any junk mail, maybe I could bring Miz Lula Maye a bouquet of wildflowers instead.

Even though the lavender was covered with teeny tiny black ants, I picked several sprigs. Miz Lula Maye says you can pull off the tiny purple flowers and tie 'em up in a handkerchief for a sachet. I ain't sure what a sachet is, but it sounds pretty. I also picked lots of white flowers with yellow centers and gold flowers with dark brown centers.

Miz Lula Maye was sitting in her rocking chair on the front porch. Mr. Window Cat was comfortably positioned on his windowsill asleep (or playin' possum). It looked like he was the only cat that had come home from the Juke Joint. That didn't surprise me. Mr. Window Cat is the oldest and, from what I've been told, the wisest of Miz Lula Maye's nine cats.

I'd been hiding the bouquet of flowers behind my back. "Happy belated birthday!" I said, holding them out in front of Miz Lula Maye.

Miz Lula Maye was so surprised. "Ain't you a sugar pie. Thank you so much, Sylvia. I loves me some flowers," she said. "Storm's brewin'. Sit down and watch it with me, child."

We sat on the porch and watched the sky. It was a weird orange-pink color with thick cotton-ball gray clouds hanging so low they could almost touch the treetops. The wind was picking up and causing the branches of the huge pecan tree in Miz Lula Maye's front yard to move like octopus arms.

"Oh, Lord," I said when a sharp flash of lightning lit up the sky. Then a loud crash of thunder roared through the muggy South Carolina air like a steam engine breaking through a glacier. A minute or two later, the rest of Miz Lula Maye's cats came runnin' home like they were crazy. Those silly cats actually left a cloud of dust behind them. It was a funny sight to see.

Miz Lula Maye shouted, "Come on, babies,

before it starts pourin' down!" Then she gave me a funny smile and said, "Cats don't like gettin' caught in the rain. Did you know that, Sylvia?" It almost seemed like she was teasing me. I was starting to wonder if Miz Lula Maye had figured out I ain't crazy about cats.

Jack Jr. dropped by to check on Miz Lula Maye. He also wanted to pass along a message from my momma asking if it would be okay if I spent the night at Miz Lula Maye's. I figured Momma didn't want me coming home in the storm. Of course, it was fine with Miz Lula Maye. And it was absolutely dy-no-mite with me!

The storm was getting closer. Jack Jr. ran for home while we lowered all the windows in the house so it wouldn't rain inside. This made the house even muggier, so Miz Lula Maye pulled out a fan to keep cool air circulating.

Suddenly, there was a blinding flash of light and a sound like firecrackers going off on the Fourth of July. Miz Lula Maye and I jumped up to look out the window. A bolt of lightning had split Miz Lula Maye's pecan tree straight across the middle. The top half of the tree had fallen over in the garden. That lightning was so close, I'm surprised it didn't set the house on fire.

Miz Lula Maye loves her big pecan tree. She sells her pecans every year at the fall town carnival, and she has already asked me if I would help her pick pecans in October. We've even planned to make pecan butter cookies. I hoped the lightning didn't do too much damage. It was nice to finally have some things to look forward to—as long as my mom decides to stay here for a while.

"It produced the biggest pecans," said Miz Lula Maye.

I could tell Miz Lula Maye was upset. "Are you okay?" I asked.

"I'll be just fine," she said. "I just hope it didn't burn down to the roots." She told me the tree would come back if its roots weren't damaged.

After the pecan tree split, Miz Lula Maye got a little nerved and decided she should let the cats in the house. When she opened the front door, there they stood, all nine of 'em, meowing and waitin' to come in and take over the house. They are so spoiled. I felt a little nerved myself with all these cats inside. They had spent the night before out in the garbage pit full of smelly fish heads and chicken parts. Was that disgusting or what!

I'd been sitting on the couch, until those darn cats took over. I like their nerve, runnin' me off the couch. I thought about taking off one of my shoes and shooing 'em away, but I didn't want Miz Lula Maye getting mad at me. After all, she was doing me a great favor by letting me spend the night. I'll get those cats one day. Maybe I'll just have to get a dog. A big, fat, mean, old, ugly, stinky, slobbering dog. Nah, I'd rather have a black female cocker spaniel. And I'd put red or pink hair ribbons on her ears. Yeah, that would be real cute.

The clouds finally decided to rain. Once it started raining real good, the roaring thunder and sharp lightning moved on by quickly. Sitting happily with Miz Lula Maye in her cucumbery-calm, dim-lighted house felt so perfect that I was fit to be tied. It was almost like make-believe. I mean, the way I felt.

Miz Lula Maye went into the kitchen to warm up supper. Jack Jr. had dropped off a big pot of stew beef with potatoes, carrots, and celery when he stopped by earlier. He actually cooks! Miz Lula Maye practically raised Jack Jr, and now he keeps an eye on her since she's so old. Aside from him always tryin' to act like a comedian, he really is a nice man.

I was surprised, but we didn't eat in the kitchen. Miz Lula Maye pulled two aluminum TV trays out of the kitchen closet. These trays fold out and stand up like little tables. She set 'em up in the front room, and we watched TV and ate supper off the TV trays. It was so much fun.

After supper, Miz Lula Maye kept watching TV and I plundered. Everything in Miz Lula Maye's house is very, very old and very interesting. Almost everything, including the people in the pictures, has a story. Most of the pictures on her wall are in black and white. Some of the pictures even look hand painted. On the fireplace mantle, behind all of Miz Lula Maye's birthday cards, sat a group picture of her family.

Miz Lula Maye had a total of nine children. Six came to the party. I'd been curious since the birthday party about how the others died. Later, when I was getting ready for bed, I asked Miz

Lula Maye to tell me who was in the picture, and she got to tellin' me all about her children.

Two children (twins, a boy and a girl) died while they were being born. Miz Lula Maye says her twins just weren't intended to be. "And Lord knows, I sho' do miss my Sara," Miz Lula Maye said. "She died tryin' to birth a son." Miz Lula Maye sighed and shook her head.

"Was she married? Did her baby live?" I asked.

"Yes, indeed," Miz Lula Maye said slowly. "Sara was married, but when she died her husband practically died from a broken heart. He couldn't bear to raise no baby, so I agreed to raise my grandson."

"Was he at your party?" I asked, trying to remember all the people I had met the night before.

"No," said Miz Lula Maye. "And I miss him as much as I miss his mother. Well, no sense in thinkin' about that."

I figure something must have happened to Miz Lula Maye's grandson. She doesn't like focusing on the dead. She states the bare facts, then explains that God brings some people into the world and quickly takes 'em out of the world. She says it is God's will and that "thy will be done." Miz Lula Maye says a lot of stuff like that. It comes from the Bible. I don't know a lot about what's in the Bible, but I do believe in God.

Miz Lula Maye turned the conversation around and began talking about something else. Since I don't remember falling asleep, I'm not sure what Miz Lula Maye was last talking about.

Chapter

SEVEN

Sunday Morning

Every Sunday, Miz Lula Maye fixes a big breakfast before going to church. The smell of fresh fish covered in cornmeal, frying in hot, salty grease was making its way into the girls' bedroom when I woke up.

I love that room. I lay there and pretended it was mine. Miz Lula Maye had told me her granddaughters and her great-granddaughters sleep in that bedroom when they come to stay. Before that, it belonged to Miz Lula Maye's daughters. It was strange how time seems to have stood still in there. A pair of Peaches's white gloves and her junior usher board name tag sat neatly arranged on a dresser. It was almost as if those items were waiting for Peaches to return.

The walls of the bedroom were covered with pictures and newspaper clippings. The wall closest to the door had a picture of Dr. Martin Luther King Jr. and a quote from his famous "I Have A Dream" speech. Miz Lula Maye's grandkids or even her great-grandkids must have put 'em there. I got out of bed and went over to get a better look.

Taped to another wall were pictures that must have been there since Miz Lula Maye's daughters were teenagers. Miz Lula Maye's girls were into music, having a good time, and dancing. Even though I've only met 'em once, I feel like I know 'em well. From the looks of the walls, they were a lively bunch. There were newspaper clippings showing people dancing at the Cotton Club and the Savoy in New York. There were pictures of Mr. Bojangles, Duke Ellington, Cab Calloway, and Count Basie.

I wondered what it would have been like to be one of Miz Lula Maye's girls. I pretended to be Peaches. She seems to fit my personality best, 'cause I love having fun. Soon I was creating rhythms of my own. My feet were tapping, I was shaking my hips, bobbing my head, and throwing my hands up and down, from side to side, front to back, a-rat-a-tat-tat. I'm throwin' down at the Juke Joint, at the Juke Joint, at the Juke Joint!

Suddenly, from the corner of my left eye, I sensed a shadow. "Child, if you don't stop that shakin' your bootie on a Sunday morning, I'm gonna have to get after you!" said Miz Lula Maye. She stood in the doorway smiling at me, wearing a gray plastic apron covered with fish scales.

"Is breakfast ready?" I asked, nearly out of breath.

"Sho' is!" said Miz Lula Maye. We both pranced into the kitchen with a frisky shuffle dance move. My eyes grew to twice their size when I saw the spread of food on the table. There was enough to feed an army.

"Come on now, Sylvia, let's sit down and bless the food," said Miz Lula Maye. "Jack Jr. will be here in a little while to take me to church." Miz Lula Maye's voice sounded a little faint. I hoped I hadn't gotten her stirred up too much with my dancing.

Then Miz Lula Maye asked in a serious or maybe I should say a concerned voice, "Sylvia, since when have you been to church?"

It had been so long since I'd been to church, I couldn't even answer her question. I just looked at her with my dark brown baby doll eyes, hoping she would invite me along. It worked.

"Well, hurry up and eat so we can get dressed," said Miz Lula Maye. I was excited, 'cause it meant that I would spend most of the day with my dearest and bestest friend, Miz Lula Maye.

Miz Lula Maye dished out the fish onto our plates. It was smokin' hot. "What kind of fish is this?" I asked.

"Catfish," said Miz Lula Maye.

I looked down at my plate. I had never seen nor eaten catfish. Why or how on earth is these fish called catfish? I thought to myself. Was it because these fish have whiskers? Did a cat and a fish get married and have babies? I was quickly losing my appetite. I messed over my food until Miz Lula Maye realized that I didn't want the catfish. She scooped it up off my plate with her hands and threw it out the back door. Her cats were already ravenously waiting at the door for leftovers. Them cats had been there all morning begging for fish. The smell of fish grease even brought in a few strays.

I figured this catfish thing out all by myself. I'm pretty sure that catfish is called catfish because they're related to cats. Those stupid cats don't know what I know. Those cats might have been eating some of their distant relatives, probably some first and second cousins. Who knows?

By the time Jack Jr. showed up, I had changed into a light pink sundress that one of Miz Lula Maye's great-granddaughters had left in a closet a few summers ago. Miz Lula Maye asked Jack Jr. to stop by my house so I could let my mom know I was going to church.

I jumped out of the car and ran into the house yelling, "Ma, Momma! I'm going to church with Miz Lula Maye and Jack Jr., if it's okay!"

Momma walked in from the kitchen. Right behind her was a man, a complete stranger, at least to me. My thoughts went crazy. Oh, my God! What in the world is a man doing in my house, with my momma? Who is he? And why is he here this time of the morning? "There's some explainin' to be done," I said suspiciously to my mother, as I looked her up and down with a sassy attitude.

Momma looked at me like I'd better straighten right up and said nothing. By then, Jack Jr. was bopping his horn for me to hurry up. I ran to the door and yelled, "I'm comin'!" I looked at the man. I looked at Momma. Then I quickly turned and pushed the screen door open. I felt my mom's hand gently rest upon my left shoulder. I held my head down as if pouting would be the most appropriate thing to do at the time.

"We'll talk after church," Momma said softly.

"You going to church?" I said, giving her this "I can't believe it" look.

Jack Jr. blew his horn as loud and long as he possibly could. I shrugged Momma's hand off my shoulder and ran out the door. I got in the car shaking my head. "The nerve of her, not letting me know her personal business!" I ranted. "I'm supposed to know this kind of stuff. I'm her one and only daughter!"

Miz Lula Maye looked worried. "Sylvia, child,"

she said. “What’s the matter, baby? You looks like you’ve seen a ghost. Does your momma not want you to go to church? Is she okay?”

Right about then, my mom and her mystery man stepped outside. Miz Lula Maye noticed ’em immediately, and so did Jack Jr. “Well, now I see the ghost you saw,” said Miz Lula Maye.

Then Jack Jr., with his silly-actin’ self, said, “Well all right, Miz Marie!” I couldn’t stand the grin on his face, so I pretended to backhand him on the head and told him to hush up about my momma.

I’d not quite seen Miz Lula Maye look like that before. I mean, I’d seen her happy, excited, mad, scared, and a little sad, but I’d never seen that look on her face. She got up out of the car and went up to the porch. “We ain’t never gonna get to church now,” I said.

The next thing I knew, Miz Lula Maye had grabbed Mr. Mystery Man and was hugging him as if she knew him. Then she hauled off and slapped the you-know-what out of him. I couldn’t believe my eyes. With no control over my mouth I said, “What the hell! Jack, did you see what Miz Lula Maye just did? I can't believe . . . Oh my! Something is goin' down. Something is rat wrong. Jack! Jack! Do you know? Who is that man?"

Jack turned around and looked at me even stupider and said, "I don't know. Wish he'd turn around so I could get a better look at his face. This is good! My Auntie Lula is m-a-d, mad!"

Jack Jr. bopped his horn and rolled down his old raggedy window. He actually suggested that we all pile up in his raggedy old car and ride to church together. Then Miz Lula Maye turned around, shaking her head no. She came back to the car saying, "We ain't goin' no place together. Take me back to the house!"

Jack Jr. finally decided to stop acting stupid and start making sense. "Auntie Maye, you need to calm right down!" he said. "We started out to church, so we's going to church!" I was in shock. I'd never heard Jack Jr. talk to Miz Lula Maye like that. Miz Lula Maye settled down, but not without a fuss.

"Auntie, why you so mad?" Jack Jr. asked.

Miz Lula Maye didn't want to talk about it,

which is the first time I've ever known Miz Lula Maye not wanting to talk about something. This must be real serious, I figured, and it must involve her in some kind of way. "Well, let's go on, then," said Miz Lula Maye in a grumpy way. "I guess I needs to go to church. I gots a lot of prayin' to do now."

I knew Miz Lula Maye was upset, but I needed to know more. "Miz Lula Maye, who is that man?" I demanded. "I got a right to know if he is withs my momma. I thought you and I were best friends. I guess I was wrong, 'cause best friends tell each other everything, both the good and the bad. So are we friends?"

Miz Lula Maye sighed. "Child, you knows we best friends," she said. "It just ain't a good time to discuss anything. My nerves is all tore up. That man, Lord, I prayed he was alive somewhere. I gots to pray and digest this." Miz Lula Maye sat back and took deep, long breaths.

"Miz Lula Maye!" I said. "Miz Lula Maye, so you do know him? Shouldn't you be happy to see someone you ain't seen in a long time?"

"I'm more than happy," she answered. "It's

just that I've wondered for so long about him and he's been alive all this time. I don't know why he didn't see fit to let me know sooner. It just makes me mad and happy all at the same time 'til I reckon I don't know how to act."

Chapter 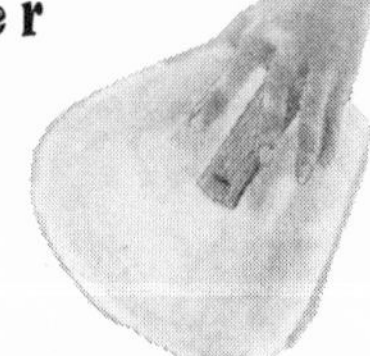 EIGHT

Visitors Please Stand

Me, Miz Lula Maye, and Jack Jr. made it to church before Momma and Mr. Mystery Man. Even though we were late, Miz Lula Maye insisted on sitting in the front middle pew the way she always does. We took our seats quickly 'cause the choir had already started singing. I turned around and spotted Momma and Mr. Mystery Man sitting in the back of the church in the last pew.

Church hasn't changed much at all since

whenever it was I last went to church. This church is actually a very large house. It has two floors. The bottom floor is where they hold the church service. There is a kitchen and a restroom at the back of the church. I figure they must do all the other church things—Sunday school and Bible study and stuff like that—upstairs.

It was some kinda hot in there. The local funeral home had supplied the church with cardboard fans, but all that fanning made me sweat even more. When it gets really hot like that, I think pastors should cancel church until it cools off.

Today during the senior choir's rendition of "Amazing Grace," one lady got so hot and happy, she fainted. Then some other people got to screamin' and shoutin' and praisin' the Lord. "Hallelujah! Hallelujah!" "Praise the Lord!" "Praise God Almighty!" three people shouted. Then one of 'em passed out on the floor. The spirit really got into a lot of people, or maybe they passed out from the heat. It's hard to say, 'cause I was so hot I felt a little weak. Nothing really moved me in church, 'cause all I could think about was that man sitting with my momma. Who ever he is, I thought, trouble must be his last name.

Just before the pastor got ready to give his final prayer and the benediction he said, "Lord, you folks are gonna have to forgive me. I forgot to recognize our visitors." I slid down in my seat as far as I could, trying my best to hide. The pastor pointed at Miz Lula Maye and said, "Sister Maye, I see you've got a visitor with you today."

I could feel Miz Lula Maye shaking like a rattlesnake. Was she shaking me? Or was she just shaking, period? I thought she was overheated, so I began fanning her as fast as I could with my cardboard fan.

Miz Lula Maye stood up and grabbed my hand, pulling me up to a standing position. Then she recognized me as her dear friend Sylvia Freeman. I didn't know what to do or say, so I didn't do or say anything. I just stood there and smiled. Then Miz Lula Maye turned around and motioned for my momma and Mr. Trouble to stand. She introduced my momma as Marie Freeman. Then Miz Lula Maye said in a trembling voice, "Church, this here is my long-lost grandson, Jonathan."

"Your what?" I exclaimed, too loud for church. "That man is your grandson?"

This had to be a dream. My mom was seeing Miz Lula Maye's grandson? Where had he been? Miz Lula Maye said he was long lost. Where was he lost and how did he find his way back? Better yet, back and with my momma, for God's sake. Skeletons were just fallin' out of the closet left and right.

After Miz Lula Maye introduced her grandson, he decided he had something to say. He stood up and looked around the room. "Church," he said, "I thank God for allowing me to come back home and worship in the house of the Lord. I am also elated (What kind of word is elated? I asked myself) to be back home to visit with my grandmother, family, and friends, and especially to meet my daughter for the first time."

Someone must have shoved a lemon down my throat, 'cause I could no longer breathe. "Is he talkin' about me, Miz Lula Maye?" I gasped. I felt lightheaded.

"Oh, my Lord!" said Miz Lula Maye. "I think

she's gonna faint. Maybe I should join her."

"Ain't this a mess?" Jack Jr. whispered, and he grabbed my shoulders and helped me sit down. I think I died for a minute or so.

When I came to, the service was over and my momma and the long-lost Mr. Jonathan were making their way up to the front pew. My heart was beating really fast, and my legs began to tremble out of control. I put my hands over my knees, trying to stop 'em from knocking, but it did no good. That's when the devil flew into me. Before I could think about what I was gonna say, I looked at Mr. Jonathan and my mouth began to move, to speak.

"Where in God's name have you been?" I demanded. (Oh, Lord! Did I say that?)

Everything in the whole world was as still as still could be. No sounds could be heard. It was like time and life stood frozen in place for a hundred years. After what I said, you would have thought I'd close my mouth. But I didn't have any control. I didn't even hear what I said 'cause more was comin' out of my mouth.

"I've been livin' ten years!" I cried. "I ain't

never got no call, no letter, no birthday card, no Christmas gift, no nothin'—absolutely nothin'! You ain't my daddy! My daddy is dead! Tell 'em, Momma! He's dead! I know he is!"

Since nothing about today had been right, I figured it would be okay for me to act like a real crazy fool. I decided to cut up real good and throw a serious temper tantrum. Yes, I, Miss Sylvia Freeman, regressed to the age of a three year old.

I grabbed the ribbon from Miz Lula Maye's great-granddaughter's old Sunday dress, yanked it from around my waist, and threw it to the floor. I was really puttin' on a star-rated show. Next, I kicked off my shoes, bent down, and Lord knows I didn't, but yes, I did. I picked up my shoes, and as hard as I could, I threw 'em straight at Mr. Jonathan's head. I didn't miss, either. Then I ran out of the church, screamin', hollerin', and cryin' like a crazy person escaping from a mental hospital.

Of course (as I intended), everyone came running after me. I headed towards the woods behind the church. I really didn't want to go back up in there by myself, so I slowed down so they could catch me.

When I first met Miz Lula Maye, she warned me not to go in those woods alone. She said there was a creek about a half a mile back that was home for all sorts of wild, dangerous animals. She said that one day I'd get to see the creek. So maybe today was that day. I didn't see why not. Everything else had happened. One more surprise wouldn't hurt anything.

Chapter  NINE

It Was the Shoes

Momma, Miz Lula Maye, and Jonathan finally made it over to me. I had stooped down under a tall oak tree, and I was out of breath after cuttin' up so. My head was drooped down as low as I could possibly hold it. I was so scared, I couldn't even look at 'em in the face. So I just looked at their shoes.

Humph! I thought. I don't see how Miz Lula Maye made it to the woods in those shoes. I'm surprised she didn't lose one.

Miz Lula Maye was wearing the ugliest dressy shoes I'd ever seen. They looked like some fancy slippers that somebody filthy rich would wear. Somebody like in Hollywood or Beverly Hills or California. First, the color—bright pinkish-orange—was all wrong. The color was so u-g-l-y, it hurt my eyes just looking. I have no idea what those shoes were made of. They kinda looked smooth, like leather, but I don't think Miz Lula Maye can afford any leather dressy shoes.

There was a bright butterfly sitting on top of each shoe, covered in what I knew wasn't diamonds. Those butterflies normally cover her toes, but looking right then, her dust-covered toes were hangin' all out and over the edge of her shoes. I figured she ought to just go barefooted.

My momma was still wearing her Sunday shoes. I like my momma's dress-up shoes. They make you taller. Why? 'Cause I believe the heels are about two or three inches high. Come to think of it, how did Momma run after me in those high heels? Her feet are small, but they looked like they were hurting. I guess chasing after me and wearing dress-up shoes don't go together.

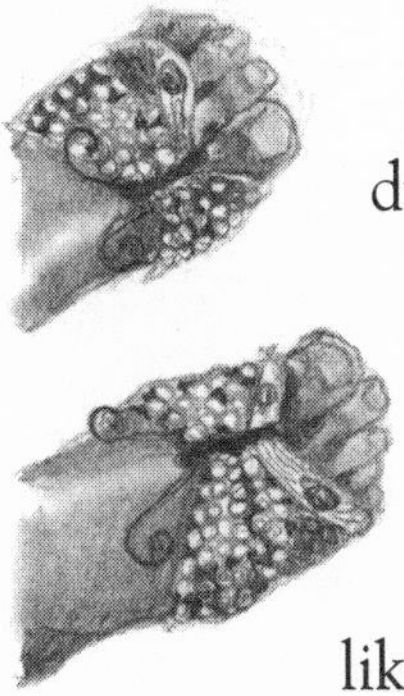

My momma is something else about her dress-up shoes. She only has two pairs. She keeps 'em in the same box she bought 'em in. That way, they stays clean and free from dust. Unfortunately, her black suede stacks with the shiny gold buckle looked like they'd been dropped in cold ashes from the bar-be-cue pit. They were completely covered in dust. I knew my momma hadn't even looked down at her feet. She hadn't even seen the shape her shoes were in, or else she would have been triple-twice as mad at me.

Then there were Jonathan's shoes (the Mystery Man). I wasn't even gonna look at his shoes, I was so mad at him. He's got some really big feet, though. And I knew that his shoes weren't leather, even though I bet he'd swear out they were. I was glad he didn't take off his "boats" and throw 'em at me. Shoes that big would cause some serious brain damage.

I was out of shoes to look at 'cause I was the only one left out there and I wasn't wearin' no shoes. Nobody was sayin' anything. They all just stood there staring at me in silence. I wanted so bad to say, "What you lookin' at? You want a piece of me?" Then I realized that maybe they were all waiting for me to look up and say something.

I'd been holding my head at the ground so long, it was too heavy for me to lift it up. In hopes of earning a little pity, I hollered, "Ouch! Ooowee Ouch! I got a cramp in my neck. I can't get up!"

With Miz Lula Maye on my right side and Momma on my left, they held me under my arms and slowly raised me up to a standing position.

That act didn't lend much sympathy.

I still hung my head low. Miz Lula Maye said, "Sylvia, child, holds your head up! Holds your head up and open your eyes. What in tarnation has gotten into you? I'm surprised! I ain't seen this Sylvia all summer."

My momma stepped in. "What did Miz Lula Maye just tell you to do?" she demanded. Then Momma yanked a long, narrow green switch from a nearby bush.

"No, Momma!" I said. I couldn't believe it. I hadn't had a whippin' in years. Momma shucked the leaves off the branch in a split second and began swingin' it at my "bee-hind." Can you believe that? I was ten years old. Too old to get a whippin'. Plus, I'm a girl! Ten-year-old girls shouldn't get whippins anymore for the rest of their life.

I'm gonna write the president of the United States and tell him to make a law that will protect ten-year-old girls from gettin' whippins. I been meaning to write the president anyway, since he didn't show up at Miz Lula Maye's one-hundredth birthday party.

Even though Momma only made contact with my butt and legs maybe eight times, she swung about eighty times. It felt like eight hundred times. I didn't know my momma could move like that, so fast-'n-all.

It was the shoes that did it, I thought. Had I not thrown my old raggedy sandals at Jonathan, the whippin' would have never happened. It was his fault. But I could tell Momma wasn't just mad at me for throwing my shoes at Jonathan. She must have also seen how messed up her Sunday shoes were.

Miz Lula Maye was not my best friend anymore, I decided. Well, at least not at that moment. A true friend would've tried to step in and stop my whippin'. Mr. Jonathan was the one. He grabbed the switch from my momma's hand and threw it out yonder like a Frisbee.

"Whew! Thank you, Jesus!" I blew with relief.

The three of 'em moved away from me a few feet to talk in private. I didn't know what they were discussing. I couldn't hear a word. My nose was itching, so I figured they must be talkin' about me. Yeah, probably so, talkin' about me.

Snot was beginning to run all out of my nose. I reckoned it was 'cause of all the screamin' and hollerin' I did during my whippin'. I didn't have any tissue, and I didn't see any trash paper around to wipe my nose. As a last resort, I raised up the hem of my dress and wiped my wet eyes, then my snotty nose. After that, I could see and breathe much better. I still didn't know what they were talkin' about, and of course, I needed to know. I mean, I should have known. I had a right to know, especially if they were talkin' about me.

That's another thing I need to write the president about. Folks shouldn't talk about other people smack in front of their face. It's just not right.

My heart was starting to beat fast again, and Lord knows, it must have been two hundred degrees outside. I made a decision. I ain't gonna say a word, I decided. I ain't. I ain't gonna say a single word.

Finally, their little meeting about yours truly was over. I was standing at guard with my arms crossed and my eyes focused straight ahead. Snot had made it to my upper lip. I could taste it. My snot had a salty, yet sweet and sweaty kind of taste. It wasn't bad. It just looked gross. Totally gross. I would have wiped it, but I didn't want to raise up my dress in front of Mr. Jonathan. That wouldn't have been ladylike. So I just let it drip.

"Sylvia, here honey," said Miz Lula Maye. "You need a napkin? Oh, here's my handkerchief. Child, wipe your nose and clean up your filthy face. It's a mess."

Well, I thought, maybe Miz Lula Maye is still a friend. Not my best friend like we was, maybe just a regular old friend. After I cleaned myself up, I handed the handkerchief back to Miz Lula Maye. She actually took it. No big deal to her. She didn't mind touching my snot. Nope, not at all. Gosh! It didn't phase her a bit. That's gross just thinkin' about it.

Miz Lula Maye nodded her head at my momma and Mr. Jonathan and said, "I'll see you all back at the house later. Take as much time as you need."

"Where are you goin', Miz Lula Maye?" I asked helplessly.

"Back to the house. You three gots a lot of

talkin' to do," Miz Lula Maye said as she slowly walked away.

OOPS! My mind stopped me. Did I just say something? I asked myself. I forgot—I ain't supposed to be talkin' anymore today.

Chapter 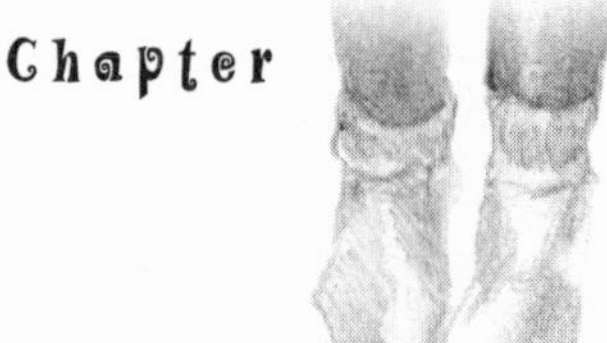 TEN

Mr. Jonathan

After Miz Lula Maye left, I finally decided to look around and see where I was. Wow! This ain't no creek back here in the woods, I realized. It's too wide and too deep to be a creek. This creek is a river.

"Sylvia, this place brings back a lot of fond memories," Mr. Jonathan said with his fancy up-North kind of talking.

Lord, I sure hope he ain't gettin' ready to share an "elating" childhood story, I said to myself. I just wasn't in the mood for listening to a stupid story from him. What I wanted to hear about was where he'd been, why he left in the first place, and what he was gonna do about things now that he was back. It's too bad I ain't talkin' anymore today, I thought, 'cause I could lay him out right now. Chew him up like Wrigley's spearmint gum and spit him out like sour milk.

My parents found a wide log to sit on. Oh, God! Oh, my God! my mind screamed. I have parents. I've never said or had parents before in my entire life! It was almost like a dream, except it was true, it was for real. No make-believe going on here, I thought, 'cause I can feel myself breathing. In dreams, you can't feel yourself breathing. You don't even know you's alive in a dream. That's why it's called a dream.

Momma motioned for me to come and sit beside her. I walked cautiously towards my p-a-r-e-n-t-s and had a seat right smack in between. I was scared and I felt alone. I guess 'cause I knew I was about to hear the truth that I'd been wondering about for all those years.

It was weird, but we just sat on that log in total silence. I finally realized that I had to be the one to get this conversation rockin'. My non-talking

spell was gonna have to be over. I decided to try to be very careful with my words and my attitude.

In a very ladylike, sweet-sounding voice, I asked, "Can we talk about things now?"

"Certainly, Sylvia!" said Mr. Jonathan with a pleasant smile.

Well now, he didn't look all that bad when he smiled. I guess earlier I hadn't noticed that Mr. Jonathan is handsome. What I had noticed earlier was that he's got some really big feet. I just hadn't noticed or paid any attention to Mr. Jonathan's long, tall body and light, almost clear brown eyes. His hair is brown, shiny, and straight. It almost looks like a white man's hair, except Mr. Jonathan is dark skinned. I would say his skin color reminds me of a milk chocolate candy bar. He has high cheeks like Miz Lula Maye's. Well, I do reckon he is Miz Lula Maye's grandson. He ought to favor her.

"Sylvia, what do you want to know first?" Mr. Jonathan asked. "Do you want to know about me and my childhood? Or do you want to hear about your mother and me?"

Again speaking very carefully, I said, "Well, I

do want to hear about you and your childhood, but not rights now. I really wants to hear about you and Momma. When ya'll met and why you left us."

Mr. Jonathan cleared his throat for a long talk. And once he got started, he talked and talked and talked.

"I met your momma at a community talent show," he said. "She was absolutely the most beautiful lady singing on stage in a quartet. Oh, sorry!" added Mr. Do-I-Look-Stupid, as if I was dumb or something. "A quartet is a singing group made up of four people."

Humpf! I thought. I already know that four people in a singing group makes up a quartet. I'm smarter than he thinks. Just 'cause I talk slang and use incomplete sentences all the time doesn't mean I don't know nothing. I got news for him. I'm a straight A student. I know how to talk grammatically proper when I'm supposed to.

"Sylvia, my eyes and your mother's eyes connected when I walked into the auditorium," said Mr. Jonathan, smiling. "Your momma had a beautiful voice."

Mr. Jonathan was a college man when he met my momma. "I was a sophomore. That means I was in my second year of college," he said.

If he doesn't stop acting like some stupid representative from *Webster's Dictionary*, I'm gonna have to go off on him! I said to myself.

He and Momma dated for a few months. They fell in love and had hopes of being together forever. At least, that's what he said. "Unfortunately, I was drafted into the army," Mr. Jonathan explained. "I got the letter one week and had to leave the very next week. We were both devastated, but there was nothing we could do."

He had to go and fight in some stupid war that ended up not being declared a war. It was called Vietnam. A lot of his friends died over in Vietnam or became "missing in action." Mr. Jonathan said that missing in action was just another way of the government saying someone is lost. This one I didn't know. Most soldiers missing in action were either dead, being held prisoner, or still hiding somewhere out there—where, only the Lord knows.

"Wow!" I said, forgetting to be careful with my

words. "That's some really sad stuff. All those young guys—their families don't know where they are or if they'll ever come home." Then I stopped and just looked at Mr. Jonathan. My daddy had come home.

I felt all strange inside. At first, I had been in shock, caught off guard, just like Miz Lula Maye was. Now I was starting to feel something different. I was starting to feel happy.

I asked if we could head back to the church. As we stood up, I took notice of another very important detail. There was no wedding ring on Mr. Jonathan's left hand. Dyn-o-mite! That was good news for my momma. But then, weren't they once married? I wondered. Huh? That's a good question. Well, if they weren't never married, maybe they might hook up. Who knows, after all these years, they might. Mr. Jonathan continued talking as we headed out of the woods. I tried my best not to miss a word he was saying.

"I wrote your mother three times," he said. "She wrote me back once, saying that she and her quartet had gotten a gig up North in a fancy dinner club. She promised that once she got settled, she would write to give me her new address." Mr. Jonathan looked at my mom. "That was the last time I heard from your momma," he said in a pitiful, cracking voice. He said he knew that being overseas, mail took three times as long to travel, but after eight months he realized he was history.

Mr. Jonathan said he didn't even know about me. He didn't even know he had a baby girl. "Now, ain't that a blip!" I whispered under my breath.

I knew my momma heard me, but I didn't even care. I couldn't believe my momma just dropped him like that. This story sounded like something off the soaps. Fred Flintstone could have come up with a better excuse. He needed to come again with a better story, 'cause I didn't buy what he was sayin' about my momma.

Then I looked at my momma. Hold up! There was no expression on her face whatsoever. No comment, no nothing was coming from her mouth. Oh no! I've figured this thing out, I realized. Mr. Jonathan was telling the truth. Momma wasn't interested in him anymore.

"Oh, Lord," I said sadly. This was going downhill

like hot lava flowing from a volcano. This was not good. Then suddenly, I wasn't happy or sad. I was mad again—madder than before. I turned back into Miss Sassy, USA.

"What happened to you?" I asked my momma.

"What?" said Momma, avoiding my question like usual. "Say what? Excuse me? Are you talking to me?" I dropped my chin to my chest like the ball dropped on New Year's Eve at Times Square. Then all of a sudden, out from nowhere, something dashed in front of us. We all stopped in our tracks instantly.

"What was that?" I whispered in holy terror.

"I think it was a deer or maybe a fox. Stand still and be quiet," whispered Mr. Jonathan. Whatever it was, it dashed back across the path. So we stood still again in silence. Then, right smack in front of our noses, about eight deer flew by. I almost wet on myself.

Mr. Jonathan pulled me back so I wouldn't get knocked down. When the deer were gone, he looked me over to make sure I was okay. He said he was used to being on guard and being prepared for the unexpected. He said that's the way you had to be every day while in Vietnam. He said you even had to be on guard in your sleep and that dreaming was something you just didn't do.

I think I understand what that must have been like.

Chapter

ELEVEN

The Best News

The silent ride home took forever. I don't know if it was Mr. Jonathan driving slow or if it was just me. As we pulled onto Pearle Road I realized I wasn't the same Sylvia Freeman that left for church this Sunday morning.

I was puzzled when Mr. Jonathan didn't drop us off at home, but instead drove all the way down Pearle Road to Miz Lula Maye's house. Jack Jr. was sittin' on the porch (surprisingly, with cats) when we pulled up. "Why are we here?" I asked.

Jack Jr. gave me a big grin and said, "We folks in Miz Lula Maye's family always eats Sunday dinner together, cousin Sylvia." His grin changed into a smirk. "You do know we is cousins now," he said, "so we can really get into some knock-down-drag-out fussin'."

"Oh, Lord," I said, rolling my eyes.

"So, Jon-Jon, what were you doing at Marie's? Is that why you're here?" asked Jack Jr.—oh, excuse me—*Cousin* Jack Jr. He was right on time. He asked the very questions I wanted to ask.

Mr. Jonathan said a light in the front window of our house caught his attention as he turned onto Pearle Road. He'd planned on surprising Miz Lula Maye, but got the real surprise when he stopped to see for himself who was living in the house.

Mr. Jonathan said he got head injuries while over in Vietnam. He lost a large part of his memory. It's hard to believe, but it has taken him nearly nine years to find his way back home. Wakeview is pretty small. If I lost my memory, it would probably take me forever to remember this place, out in the middle of nowhere. Mr.

Jonathan claimed he recognized my momma immediately when she opened the door. He said seeing her face turned on a million lights in his head.

When my mom and dad walked into the kitchen, everything went quiet. I felt strange and out of place for the first time in Miz Lula Maye's house. Then Miz Lula Maye began laughing for no reason. Jack Jr. and Mr. Jonathan started laughing, too. Everybody was so nervous, me triply included. Surely, I had been dropped off at the lu-lu nut farm, I thought. What was so funny?

Miz Lula Maye said, "We sho' have a lot of explainin' and talkin' to do, but let's eat first. Come on, Sylvia, and help your great-grandma serve dinner."

Well, that's what I did. I don't know when Miz Lula Maye cooked all that food, but there once again, she had another full table. From left to right going straight across, I saw golden brown cornbread sticks, shaped like little ears of corn; a bowl of field peas, which looked almost like black-eyed peas except they were kinda green in color; a plate of fried okra; and a pot of white rice with salted country ham and black pepper sitting on top.

In the middle of the table sat a huge country ham laid out on a beautiful white porcelain serving platter. Beside the ham was a bowl of Miz Lula Maye's world-famous potato salad, which has crispy pieces of cucumber in it. Next was a bowl of fresh fried spring onions and catfish fritters, which look like pancakes. Four melt-in-your-mouth, buttery sweet potato pies were sitting over on the counter beside the sink. We all sat down and ate entirely too much Sunday supper.

I thought there was supposed to be so much talking and catching up that needed to be done. But there I was, sitting in Miz Lula Maye's front room watching overstuffed grown-ups sleep in the afternoon.

Even though everybody was in shock at first, now they all seemed glad to see this man who is also my daddy. Just look at 'em! I thought.

Jack Jr. was sitting on the couch beside my momma. He was so knocked out, the red, black, and green pick stuck in the left side of his 'fro was about to fall out.

Most of the time when I look at Jack Jr. I can't help but smile. True, he gets on my last nerve, but he is so funny. Jack Jr.'s always got something going on. I was having to keep myself from busting out laughing. Why? 'Cause Jack Jr. was chewing in his sleep. He looked like a horse, or better yet, a cow. A lazy, old, ugly cow.

My first mind told me to go over and mess with Jack Jr. but my momma's left eye cracked open before I could make my move. Then Mr. Jonathan started to wiggle and yawn like he was getting ready to wake up. Next, Miz Lula Maye made this kinda grunt-snort-sniff sound. She rubbed her nose with a lace-trimmed linen handkerchief folded in her right hand and let out a loud high-pitched sneeze.

My momma nudged Jack Jr., then signaled for me to come and sit on the couch with her. "Move over, Jack, and let Sylvia sit beside me," Momma said.

Jack Jr. tried to pretend like he was asleep and didn't hear her. So she said it again, trying to be a little quiet since Miz Lula Maye was still kinda dozing in and out. "Jack, I said move over. I know you hear me." But Jack Jr. didn't budge.

We all thought Miz Lula Maye was still asleep, but little did we know she was playin' possum. Miz Basket Cat was asleep in Miz Lula Maye's lap, curled up in a tight letter C. After Jack Jr. wouldn't move so I could sit beside my momma, Miz Lula Maye up and tossed Miz Basket Cat right onto Jack Jr.'s lap.

During her short flight, Miz Basket Cat let out a loud "Meee-ooo-www-scc-reee-chhh!" It scared the field peas right out of Jack Jr. It kinda scared me, too. For sure, everybody was definitely awake, especially stupid-acting Jack Jr. and Miz Lula Maye's other eight cats.

Jack Jr. got to fussin' with Miz Lula Maye. On his way to the bathroom he said, "Why did you have to go sickin' one of your cats on me? One of these days . . . "

"One of these days what?" said Miz Lula Maye in a come-right-back-at-ya voice. "What you gonna do? One of these days nothin'. You ain't never gonna touch any of my cats 'cause you knows good and well you ain't wantin' to have to deal with me. So take your scruffy little behind on in the bathroom and hush up! And don't stink it up in there, either!"

Jack Jr., having to have the last word, shouted from the bathroom, "I want my spot back on the couch when I come out of here!" Miz Lula Maye laughed.

It's some kinda funny listening to those two get at each other. They fuss more than a married couple. You can tell they love each other, though. I guess that's how it is with family.

Finally, I made it over to the couch, taking over Jack Jr.'s spot. I snuggled up under my momma's right underarm. My momma smelled like those lavender wildflowers that grow by the road. It's a nice, sweet, soft, and earthy kind of smell. I declare, every time I smell that smell, it calms and relaxes me on the inside. It's strange for a smell to do that, but it does. I feel at ease or comfortable when I smell that lavender smell. I never considered this before, but maybe it works that way 'cause it smells like my momma.

I wish my momma was still in love with Mr. Jonathan so I could have a daddy, too. But maybe I could have a daddy even if he wasn't married to my momma. I don't know. I'll have to figure that out. Right then, I had other things to figure out.

I cleared my throat about eight times. It felt like the same lemon from church was stuck in my throat again. Mr. Jonathan politely asked, "Are you okay, Sylvia?" I cleared my throat again and slowly said, "Yes sir, I'm okay."

I got up from the sofa and walked over to Miz Lula Maye. Then I asked a very brave question. "Miz Lula Maye, now that I'm your great-granddaughter and you're my great-grandma, how can we still be friends?"

I started to cry. This was too much for a ten-year-old to handle. It was way too confusing. I honestly didn't know what to say or think.

Miz Lula Maye settled me down by hugging me with a gentle swaying from side to side. Then she said, "Sylvia, childs, the Lord knows I loves you. Everybody knows I loves me some Sylvia,

and whether you my great-granddaughter or not, we was friends first, so we'll always be friends, the best of friends 'til the end. And when we gets to heaven, we'll be friends there, too. We'll water wildflowers with our tears of joy. Now ain't that just the best news you ever heard?"

ACKNOWLEDGMENTS

Much love and gratitude goes to all of my family, and to the memory of my father. Thank you a million times to my husband, Merrill, and my children, Jasmine and Joey, for listening to my stories. To my mom, Zelene Hart, thank you for your love, spirit, faith, and strength. You are my wings. To my brothers, Boyd, Sonny, and Tony, and my sisters, Pat, Ernestine, and Gwen, thanks for always "backing up" your little sister.

Thank you to everyone at Carolrhoda Books. A special thanks to my editor, Vicki Liestman. You are so, so wonderful! And Gar Willets, thanks for answering my one thousand questions. What can I say about an artist whose work speaks for itself? Thanks Felicia Marshall for illustrating my first novel.

Last, but certainly not least, thank you Mr. Lawrence Eppes, Mrs. Sandra Gemach, and Mr. "A" (Alexander) for your artistic influence. You will always be remembered as my favorite childhood teachers.